Planet
of the
Penguins

To RoseMary Hunt,
With infinite thanks for your math expertise —D.L.

To Caleb. THANK YOU for your guidance, support,
knowledge, and humor. —M.G.

STERLING CHILDREN'S BOOKS
New York

An Imprint of Sterling Publishing Co., Inc.
1166 Avenue of the Americas
New York, NY 10036

STERLING CHILDREN'S BOOKS and the
distinctive Sterling Children's Books logo are registered trademarks
of Sterling Publishing Co., Inc.

Text © 2019 David LaRochelle
Illustrations © 2019 Mike Gorman

ISBN 978-1-4549-2922-2

Distributed in Canada by Sterling Publishing Co., Inc.
c/o Canadian Manda Group, 664 Annette Street
Toronto, Ontario M6S 2C8, Canada
Distributed in the United Kingdom by GMC Distribution Services
Castle Place, 166 High Street, Lewes, East Sussex BN7 1XU, England
Distributed in Australia by NewSouth Books
University of New South Wales, Sydney, NSW 2052, Australia

For information about custom editions, special sales, and premium and
corporate purchases, please contact Sterling Special Sales at 800-805-5489 or
specialsales@sterlingpublishing.com.

Manufactured in Canada

Lot #:
2 4 6 8 10 9 7 5 3 1
09/19

sterlingpublishing.com
Cover and interior design by Irene Vandervoort

ALIEN MATH SERIES
Book Number Two

Planet OF THE Penguins

by DAVID LaROCHELLE
illustrated by MIKE GORMAN

STERLING CHILDREN'S BOOKS
New York

CHAPTER 1

A Surprise Reunion

Math can be dangerous. It can also be feathery, wet, and smelly. Trust me, I know.

At the moment, math was being delicious. My best friend, Lamar Wilson, and I were sitting at my kitchen table. We were *supposed* to be studying our spelling words, but instead we were eating brownies and making up math problems.

"If I want to divide a pan of brownies into twenty-four equal bars, how many different ways can I do that using only horizontal and vertical cuts?" asked Lamar.

Lamar and I both like math. A *lot*. In fact, we're co-captains of our school's Math All-Stars team. We won our first tournament of the year last Saturday answering problems just like the one Lamar had made up. I was predicting an undefeated season.

I took another brownie from the pan that Lamar's mother had baked, then visualized all the ways I could divide the pan of brownies into twenty-four equal pieces:

6 rows with 4 brownies in each row
4 rows with 6 brownies in each row
8 rows with 3 brownies in each row
3 rows with 8 brownies in each row
12 rows with 2 brownies in each row
2 rows with 12 brownies in each row

That was six different ways.

I was about to give Lamar my answer, but this seemed too easy. Knowing Lamar, he'd try to trick me.

I kept thinking. Then I pictured another possibility: 24 rows made up of just one brownie, or 1 row divided into 24 brownies. The brownies would look like long, skinny, over-cooked French fries, but I'd have twenty-four and they would all be equal.

"Eight different ways," I told Lamar.

"Stupendous!" he said. *Stupendous* was one of our spelling words. "Now it's your turn, Lexie. Go ahead, try to stump me."

I licked a crumb of chocolate from my finger as I thought of a real challenge for Lamar.

"If it takes a person six bites to eat one brownie, and if you take three bites for every one bite that I take, then how many brownies will we . . ."

"Wait a minute!" said Lamar. "I do *not* eat three times as fast as you do!"

He definitely does. I'm good at noticing details like that.

I pointed at the pan that was already one-third empty. "We had better *both* slow down eating," I told him. "Your mom made us promise we'd leave plenty of brownies for my dad."

My dad eats brownies twice as fast as Lamar. That means six times faster than I do.

"Leaving brownies for your father is an honorable thought," said Lamar, "so I will take only one more brownie for mental inspiration." *Honorable* and *inspiration* were also spelling words.

As Lamar's hand reached for the pan, a blinding flash of green light filled the kitchen. For seven seconds my ears rang with the sound of crackling and popping fireworks. When the crackling stopped, we were no longer in my kitchen. In fact, we were no longer in our apartment building or even on planet Earth.

Lamar and I were standing inside a gleaming spaceship looking down at a shaggy purple alien with six legs and ping-pong ball eyes perched on top of three-inch-long antennae.

Most people would have freaked out.

Not us.

"Fooz? Is that really you?" I said.

"Wow! I never thought we'd see you again!" added Lamar.

A month ago (thirty-four days, to be exact), Fooz had beamed us aboard her spaceship. We had some *really* strange adventures on a planet called Flacknar before we figured out how to get back home again.

"Yes, yes," said Fooz in her squeaky, high-pitched voice. "It is a very good thing to see the two of you also."

"What brings you back to our galaxy?" I asked. "Are you still searching for exotic animals?"

"Oh . . . no . . . no . . . I . . . uh . . . I just happened to be in

your vicinity . . . and I thought I would visit my two favorite Earthlings."

Fooz shifted back and forth on her feet seven times while talking. Her ping-pong ball eyes looked in every direction but at us, and both of her tails twitched nervously. She might have been super-smart, but she wasn't very good at lying.

"C'mon, Fooz," said Lamar. "What's up?"

"You are correct," she said, finally looking us in the eyes. "There is another reason why I am here. But it is a difficult thing for me to say."

"What is it?"

Fooz took a deep breath.

"My home planet of Zan is in grave danger. The life of every Zanarian is in peril. I am hoping that the two of you will lend us your assistance."

I had never seen Fooz look so serious.

"That's awful!" I said.

"What's the terrible danger?" asked Lamar.

Fooz took an even deeper breath.

"My planet has been invaded by . . . penguins."

Lamar laughed. I almost did, too.

"Sorry, Fooz," said Lamar, "but for a second I thought you said your planet was invaded by *penguins*."

"Yes, yes, that is exactly what I said."

"But penguins aren't dangerous," I replied.

"I am relieved that you feel that way," said Fooz, "but the inhabitants of my planet feel differently. In fact, we are

terrified of penguins. If a Zanarian even *sees* a penguin, the molecules in his body reacts so strongly that the Zanarian is turned to stone." Fooz shuttered from her eyeballs to the tips of her tails.

"I remembered how skillfully you dealt with the creatures on Planet Zacknar. We now need your cleverness on my planet. I was hoping you'd be willing to help us deal with these frightening creatures." She looked at us with pleading eyes.

It felt good that Fooz thought the two of us were so smart. And if she had traveled all this way for our help, how could we say no?

I glanced at Lamar. He was already wearing the excited look he gets before a math tournament. We exchanged quick nods.

"Bring on the penguins!" he said.

"Thank you, thank you!" exclaimed Fooz, clapping her front two hands/feet together. "You cannot understand how important this is to us. Our entire planet will be grateful!" She hurried over to the control panel of her ship. "There is no time to lose. The penguins' spaceship landed outside of my planet's capital city of Naznar this morning. With each passing minute we worry that the penguins will disembark and the life of every Zanarian will be threatened."

"Have you tried talking with them yet?" asked Lamar. "Maybe if you just asked them to leave, they'd go away."

"That is exactly where the two of you come in," said Fooz. "But I will let the leader of the Zanarian Security Council explain all of that to you. She will be as relieved as I am to hear of your help."

Fooz stood up on her back legs and pressed a green rectangular button on her spaceship's control panel. A large monitor appeared in front of us.

"The leader of our security council is Zellen-Eez-Wanna-Walla-Locken-Dorn-Dar, but as I recall, you Earth-lings have trouble with such long names. Let me reduce that by 87.5 percent. You may simply call her Zell."

Fooz adjusted a knob, and an image appeared on the screen. It showed a square-shaped room with a large round table. Behind the table hung a blue-and-gold square flag with three concentric circles. In the small center circle was a large gold Z. The room was empty.

"This is very unusual," muttered Fooz. "Zellen-Eez-Wanna-Walla-Locken-Dorn-Dar was at the Zanarian Security Chamber just minutes ago. She assured me that she would wait there until I contacted you."

Suddenly a tiny black-and-white head peeked over the edge of the table. It had shiny black eyes and a short pointed beak.

"It's a baby!" I exclaimed. "A little baby penguin!"

"Is this one of your dangerous invaders?" asked Lamar. "That little fellow doesn't look scary at all!"

I agreed. This creature looked like something you'd want to pick up and cuddle, like a six-week-old kitten.

But Fooz didn't answer. When we looked down, we discovered why.

Her mouth was wide open and she was staring at the screen. But she wasn't screaming. She stood completely motionless. That's because her entire body had turned to solid gray stone.

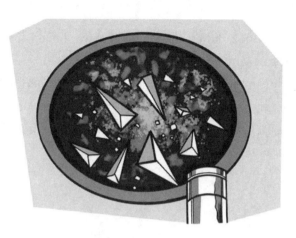

CHAPTER ½ + ½ + ½ + ½

Outer Space Emergency

"**F**ooz!"

I knelt down and placed my hands on her shaggy body. It was as cold and hard as our front steps on the thirty-seventh day of winter.

"What did you do to her?" I yelled at the screen, but the baby penguin had disappeared and the monitor was blank.

"Fooz, can you hear us?"

Lamar waved his hands in front of her eyes. He snapped his fingers, then clapped his hands like our math teacher does when she wants to get our attention.

No response.

I gently shook Fooz back and forth, hoping she would snap out of the trance or spell or whatever had been triggered by seeing the penguin, but she remained stiff and cold.

14

"How could this happen?" I asked. Lamar didn't say anything, but he looked as worried as I felt.

"Do you think Fooz has a first-aid kit on her ship? If she does—" but the rest of my sentence was cut off by a loud buzzing alarm and a bright red light that flashed overhead.

Our troubles were about to double.

"Warning," announced a harsh mechanical voice. "Ice storm approaching. Adjust course now or prepare for impact in 8.3 minutes."

Lamar and I looked out the window. Far in the distance we saw a white smudge in the deep black of outer space. It was only the size of a golf ball, but it was getting bigger.

I was about to ask Fooz how badly an ice storm could damage her ship, but then I realized she couldn't answer. Worse, she couldn't adjust our course to avoid a collision.

"We'll have to deal with Fooz later," said Lamar. "Right now we need to get out of the path of that ice storm or all three of us will be in trouble. Lexie, you check the control panel and see if you can find a way to steer this spaceship. I'm going to use Fooz's monitor to find someone to help us."

Lamar is good at taking charge and making a plan of action. That's what makes him such a valuable co-captain of our school's math team. I'm good at noticing details that others overlook, and that's what makes *me* such a valuable co-captain. If we ever needed both of our skills, it was now.

I turned my attention to the spaceship's control panel. It was five feet long and two feet wide. It was covered with brightly lit buttons, knobs, and screens in every shape

imaginable: trapezoids, rhombuses, pentagons, nonagons ... even a few shapes that I couldn't identify. The first thing I did was look for a joystick or steering wheel, but there wasn't one.

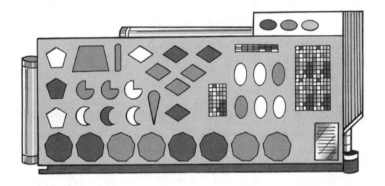

"Warning," announced the mechanical voice. "Ice storm approaching. Adjust course *immediately*, or prepare for impact in 6.2 minutes."

I shot a quick glance out the window. The white smudge was now the size of a soccer ball. I could make out individual ice chunks spinning through space. They were sharp and pointed, like obtuse triangles, and they looked as deadly as shards of broken glass.

Lamar was rapidly adjusting knobs on the monitor. He had succeeded in bringing the Zanarian Security Chamber back on the screen, but the baby penguin was gone and no one was answering his calls for help.

I turned my attention back to the control panel. Most of the buttons weren't labeled, and randomly hitting knobs

didn't seem like a smart idea. Then, in the lower right corner, I spotted a metal plate the size of a playing card. It read:

In case of an emergency, follow these instructions in order:

1. *If Dial A is < Dial D, change Dial C to 3 more than Dial B.*
2. *If Dial B is > Dial A, change Dial D to 1 less than Dial A.*
3. *If the difference between Dial A and Dial B is an even number, then change Dial A to 4 less than Dial B. If the difference is an odd number, change Dial B to 4 more than Dial A.*
4. *Pull the green lever.*

Below the panel were four small dials labeled *A*, *B*, *C*, and *D*. They were currently set at 7, 16, 14, and 28.

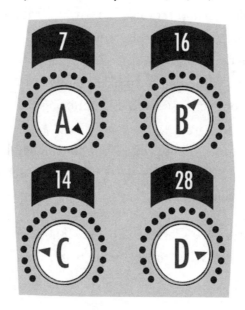

The bright red light began flashing faster. "Warning!" announced the mechanical voice. "Evacuate the ship, or prepare for collision with ice storm in 1.5 minutes."

That was only ninety seconds!

Knowing I couldn't afford to make a mistake, I took a calming breath and tried to ignore the blaring alarm. Step by step, I carefully followed the first three lines of the instructions. When the dials were set, I grabbed the green lever and pulled it down hard.

Lamar and I were thrown to the floor. Fooz toppled onto her side. The inside of the spaceship went dark, and a scorching white light flooded through the window. The entire ship shook like a runaway roller-coaster car for five minutes and twelve seconds. (I timed it on my watch.)

Then just as suddenly, the shaking stopped. The alarm went silent. The light outside the ship vanished, and the lights inside the ship returned. Lamar and I didn't move, waiting to see if something else would happen.

It didn't.

Lamar was the first to speak. "I don't know what you did, Lexie, but you just saved us from being pulverized by that ice storm."

I wasn't exactly sure what I had done either, but I was glad we were still alive. The steps I had taken to set the dials must have been correct:

- Dial A (7) was less than Dial D (28), so I had changed Dial C to 19 (3 more than 16).

- Dial B (16) was greater than Dial A (7), so I had changed Dial D to 6 (1 less than 7).
- The difference between Dial A (7) and Dial B (16) was an odd number (9), so I changed Dial B to 11 (4 more than 7).

The settings 7, 11, 19, and 6 had saved our lives.

The first thing we did was check on Fooz. Lamar set her back on her six feet, and we checked to make sure she was still in one piece. Nothing had broken off, and neither of us spotted any cracks or chips in her solid stone body.

Then we looked out the elliptical window, but all we saw was a flat silver sky.

"It doesn't feel like the spaceship is moving," said Lamar. "Maybe we've landed." He glanced around the ship. "How do you think we get out?"

"That's easy," I said.

I remembered the button Fooz had used on our last trip. It was located next to a dial that indicated the air quality outside the ship. The dial was pointing to the safe zone, so I tapped the button three times just as I had seen Fooz do. A triangular door slid open, and Lamar and I peered out through the opening.

I expected to be looking out at a strange planet. Instead, the spaceship was inside a very large room. It was as wide as two school buses parked end to end and three times as long. The walls, ceiling, and floor were all made of gleaming silver metal. The window of Fooz's spaceship was

only inches away from one of the walls, which was why we couldn't see anything else when we had looked out. The rest of the room was filled with other spaceships. It looked like a parking lot for extraterrestrials.

Lamar cupped his hands around his mouth. "Hello!" he called. "Anybody here? We need some help for our friend!"

Nobody answered except a hollow echo.

"If we want help, it looks like we're going to have to go out and find it," he said.

I hated to leave Fooz by herself, but I knew Lamar was right. Before leaving the spaceship, we both knelt beside her.

"We'll be back," I said. "We promise."

"And we'll find a way to change you back from stone," said Lamar. "Count on it."

I wished I felt as confident as Lamar sounded.

We climbed down the ramp and began walking toward the center of the long room with spaceships on either side of us. The only sound was the slapping of our tennis shoes on the metal floor.

"Do you notice anything strange about all these ships?" I asked.

"Well, for one thing," said Lamar, "they all look exactly alike."

"Even more than that," I said. "They all look exactly like Fooz's ship. They're the same size, the same color, and they even have the same insignia drawn on their sides: three concentric circles with a Z in the middle. That was the symbol we saw on the flag in the Zanarian Security Chamber. I think we've landed on Fooz's home planet of Zan."

"I bet you're right," said Lamar. "But if that's the case, where are all the Zanarians?"

That's when we spotted someone up ahead. In fact, it looked like a cluster of creatures, all the size of Fooz.

"Hello!" shouted Lamar, waving his hands.

They didn't answer or wave back.

"Maybe they're too far away to hear," I said.

We took off jogging in their direction, but as we got closer, we slowed down. When we were twenty feet away, my heart sank to the bottom of my feet.

The reason why these Zanarians hadn't answered was because they had all been turned to stone.

I counted eight of them. They looked just like Fooz: shaggy fur, six legs, two tails. But what made the hair on the back of my neck bristle was the terrified look on their faces. Their mouths were wide open, and their eyes were staring in the same direction.

We followed their gaze to a cube-shaped structure against the wall. It was a yard long on each side. The side closest to us was open.

"It looks like an old-fashioned phone booth," said Lamar, "for very short people."

"Or for creatures the size of Fooz," I said.

We ducked down to look inside. From the frozen expressions on these Zanarians' faces, I expected to see a penguin inside the cube. But the cube was empty. Well, almost empty.

On the back wall of the cube was a 9 × 9 grid covered with shapes and letters. The grid was labeled *City of Naznar.*

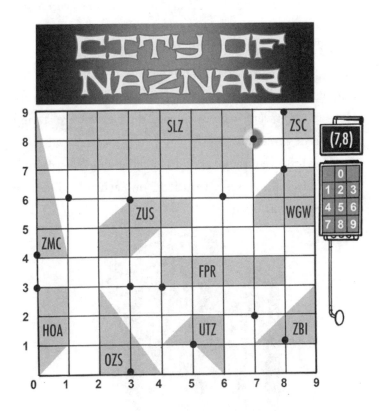

"Naznar is the capital of Fooz's planet," I said, remembering what Fooz had told us back in the ship. "And this must be a map of the city."

Alongside the map was a numerical keypad, with buttons labeled 0 through 9. The digital display above the keypad showed the numbers 7 and 8 in parentheses separated by a comma. Remembering what we had learned about using coordinate grids, I put my finger on the 0 at the bottom of the grid, and slid it along the horizontal line until I reached the vertical line labeled 7. Then I slid my finger up the line till I reached the horizontal line labeled 8. At that intersection, a tiny blue light no bigger than a pencil point glowed.

"If this is a map, then that must be the spot where we're standing," said Lamar.

It made sense. The blue light was at the far end of a large rectangle that was three times longer than it was wide. Those were the same proportions as the building we were in right now.

"Hmmmm," he said. "I wonder what happens if we enter a *different* set of coordinates?"

The map was spotted with a lot of other dots that weren't glowing. Most of them were touching the side of a building.

"If this is a phone booth," I said, "then maybe if we enter the coordinates for a dot touching a building, we can talk with the creatures in that room."

"Possibly . . . ," said Lamar. I detected a fraction of excitement creeping into his voice. "Or maybe it's *not*

a phone booth Maybe it's a transport cube. If we enter another pair of coordinates, maybe we'll be transported to that spot."

My skin prickled as if I had been tickled with 144 toothbrushes. I had read about transport machines in books and had seen them in science-fiction movies, but I never thought they were real.

"There's only one way we'll ever find out what happens," said Lamar. He poised his finger over the keypad. "What two numbers should we try?"

That was a very good question. I counted thirteen different dots on the map, not including the blue dot where we were now. I also noticed that the ten different buildings were each labeled with three letters, but I didn't know what the letters meant.

We knew we needed to stop the penguins. And we knew that Zell had a plan for us. But we *didn't* know where we should go to get help.

"If this cube really *is* a transport machine," said Lamar, "let's try the coordinates (8, 9)."

I checked the map, and gave Lamar the thumbs-up sign.

"Excellent choice!" I told him. From the information that Fooz had given us before she was turned to stone, I knew that this was the perfect spot to begin our search.

CHAPTER 6 × ? = 39 – 21

Cryptic Clues

The coordinates (8, 9) pointed to a spot at the corner of a square building labeled *ZSC*.

ZSC.

The Zanarian Security Chamber.

That's the room where the baby penguin had appeared on Fooz's screen. We needed to stop the penguins, and this was a logical place for us to start.

"Hang on," said Lamar. "Let's see if this machine can take us there."

He punched the numbers 8 and 9 into the keypad. I braced myself for a rush of wind or the rattling and shaking we had experienced when I pulled the emergency lever on Fooz's spaceship. But I didn't feel any of that.

"Dang," said Lamar. "I guess this isn't a transport machine after all. Nothing happened."

"Yes it did," I said pointing at the map. "The blue dot has changed." Now the bright blue dot was at the point (8, 9).

We backed out of the cube and looked at our new surroundings. We were no longer inside the storage building for spaceships; instead, we were in the corner of a square room with a round table in the center and the Zanarian flag hanging against one of the walls. It was the room we had seen on Fooz's monitor.

What we *hadn't* noticed on the monitor was that the room was a mess. The table was scattered with papers and strange writing instruments. Several of the benches surrounding the table had been knocked over.

We did not, however, see the baby penguin.

"It looks like someone left in a hurry," said Lamar.

"And it looks like someone didn't make it in time," I added sadly. Huddled under the table was another Zanarian. She, too, had been turned to stone.

I was beginning to worry that we were too late to save *anyone* on Fooz's planet when I noticed a strange odor.

"Eww," I said, sniffing the air. "What's that smell?" The air held the faint aroma of salmon. It's my least favorite food by a factor of 9.

We heard a soft shuffling sound. Then a little baby penguin crawled out from behind one of the benches where it had been hiding. It had a black-and-white head and was covered with fluffy gray feathers.

"Peep!" it said in a tiny voice.

It flapped its little flippers and blinked its tiny black

eyes. How could something so cute be causing so much trouble?

"Boy, am I glad we found you!" said Lamar. "Don't you realize what you're doing? You've got to stop turning these Zanarians to stone!"

"Peep!" said the penguin again. It shook its head back and forth. Did that mean, "No, I'm not going to stop turning the Zanarians to stone"? Or did it mean, "No, I have absolutely no idea what you're telling me"?

The penguin stretched its neck upward and then pulled a sheet of paper from the edge of the table with its beak.

"Hey, put that back!" said Lamar.

The penguin backed away from us, dragging the paper with it.

I took a step forward. "Don't worry," I said, "we won't hurt you. But let us take a look at what you've got."

The penguin crawled beneath the table. We got down on our hands and knees to find it, but it was hard to see around the overturned benches.

"Hey!" said Lamar. "It's getting away!"

The penguin had crawled out from the other side of the table and was heading toward the transport cube.

"Wait! Don't go!"

We ran for the penguin but couldn't reach it before it waddled into the cube. Then it reached as high as it could and slapped the bottom row of buttons with its little flippers. Just like that, it vanished and the transport cube was empty, except for the penguin's fishy smell.

"What a sneaky little troublemaker," said Lamar.

We checked the digital display above the keypad, hoping it would show us where the penguin had gone. It didn't. It only displayed the coordinates for the room we were in now: (8, 9).

"At least the penguin dropped this before it reached the cube," I said, picking up the paper it had been dragging. I held it up so Lamar and I could both read it at the same time.

To: Foozen-Allwyn-Crypto-Noomin-Regan-Zenar-Mush-Mush

From: Zellen-Eez-Wanna-Walla-Locken-Dorn-Dar

If you are reading this, then my fears have come true. The members of the security council have all been turned to stone, and we were not able to meet with you in person to discuss our plans for the protection of our planet. This letter, however, will tell you everything you need to know to save the rest of the inhabitants of Zan.

I trust you have returned with help from another planet. The first thing they will require is translation devices so that they can communicate with the penguins.

Earlier today I stored these devices in a building with a floor space that is three times the area of the Zanarian Security Chamber. The translators will be hidden there safely until you arrive.

Once you have found the vault where they are

stored, take a careful look at these words: TWENTY-FIVE IS NEVER COUNTED LIKE SIX.

As soon as your friends have the translators, it will be up to them to—

That's where the note ended.

"That must have been when the penguin arrived," I said.

"At least we know what our next step is," said Lamar. "We need to find those translators so we can talk to the penguins and stop them from destroying this planet."

That meant finding a building with floor space three times larger than where we were now. We both knew that area means the surface space of a flat object. It was easy to figure out the area of the Zenarian Security Chamber by looking at the grid in the transport cube. The building covered exactly one square unit. We needed to find a building that covered exactly *three* square units in size.

We eliminated most of the other buildings on the map by simply counting how many squares and half squares they covered. That left us with two buildings: ZMC and OZS. I estimated that each one covered *about* three squares, but it was hard to tell for sure.

"How can we tell which one is exactly three square units in size?" I said.

"Easy," said Lamar. "Here's something I learned from my dad. Watch."

Lamar's father is a university math teacher. He's given us lots of tips that help prepare us for our math tournaments.

With his finger, Lamar traced a rectangle on the grid that went from (0, 4) to (1, 4) to (1, 9) to (0, 9).

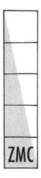

"Okay, Lexie. What's the area of this rectangle?" he asked.

"Simple," I said counting. "Five square units."

"Right. And if you divide the rectangle in half diagonally, that's how much space building ZMC covers. Its area is half of the rectangle: two and a half square units."

That *was* easy.

Using the same strategy, we found it was just as easy to determine the area of building OZS. I made an imaginary rectangle from (2, 0) to (4, 0) to (4, 3) to (2, 3).

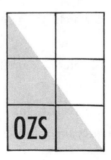

The area of the rectangle was six square units. The shaded space occupied by building OZS was half of that, so its area was three square units.

We had found our building!

We climbed back into the transport cube, and in less time than it takes to multiply a number by 10, we were in a large three-sided room. It was difficult to see much at first because the room was lit by a strange red light. When my eyes adjusted, I saw that all three walls were lined with shelves. The shelves were stacked with crates and chests. The room must not have been used much, because everything was covered with a fine coating of silvery dust.

Lamar let out a long sigh. "Zell didn't make this easy. This place is more packed than the storeroom at our apartment building."

OZS. I bet that stood for Official Zanarian Storeroom!

"If that vault is hidden behind one of these crates," Lamar continued, "it could take us hours to find it." He walked to one end of the longest wall and moved a box aside. "Well, the sooner we start looking, the sooner we'll find the vault."

I did some quick mental estimating. There were eight long shelves on each of the three walls. I estimated there were about thirty boxes or crates on each of the shelves. That meant there were . . . approximately 720 things to look behind!

Lamar was right. It *would* take a long time to search this storeroom, especially since some of the shelves were over our heads and hard to reach.

Then I noticed something else. Lamar's tennis shoes were leaving soft footprints in the dust. And there was another set of footprints leading from the transport cube as well. They weren't webbed, like a penguin's foot, but there were a lot of them. Perhaps they were made by a creature with a lot of feet—perhaps made by a Zanarian, like Zell. I followed the footprints from the transport cube to a shelf a few feet away. Where the footprints stopped, I slid aside a tall crate.

Eureka!

Set into the wall behind the crate was a small hexagonal door.

"Way to go, Lexie!" said Lamar when he saw what I had uncovered. "Excellent detective work!" We exchanged our math team's victory cheer, a triple high five.

I grabbed the handle to the vault and pulled, but the door didn't open. Neither of us was surprised.

Alongside the door in a vertical column were six round dials. Each dial was labeled 1 to 100.

"*Twenty-five is never counted like six*," said Lamar, remembering the clue in Zell's note. "It sounds like a riddle. What could be 'counted like six'?"

"Well, there are six dials on the wall," I said.

"And six sides to the vault," added Lamar. "But I don't see twenty-five of anything."

"There are also six words in her clue," I said. "Maybe if we set each dial to the number of letters in each clue word, that might open the door."

I counted the letters in the six words while Lamar set the dials to 10, 2, 5, 7, 4, and 3. He pulled on the vault's handle and . . . it still wouldn't budge.

What were we missing about her clue?

I took a look at the note again . . . and I'm glad that I did. When I looked at her writing in the glow of the red light, her clue looked different. Some of the letters in each word were glowing:

TWENTY-FIVE IS NEVER COUNTED LIKE SIX.

I showed the note to Lamar.

"Sweet!" he said. He wrote the highlighted letters in the dust on the floor.

When I saw them, I recognized them immediately. So did Lamar.

And when we recognized them, the way to opening the vault was as simple as kindergarten homework.

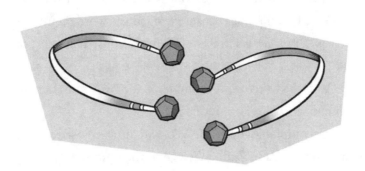

CHAPTER 1.69 + 2.31

Searching for Penguins

The glowing letters were Roman numerals:

IV, I, V, C, LI, IX

I had seen most of the numerals on the face of the old-fashioned clock hanging in our apartment's lobby. It was easy to translate their values:

$$IV = 4$$
$$I = 1$$
$$V = 5$$
$$IX = 9$$

I traced the familiar Arabic numbers in the dust beneath their Roman counterparts.

I also knew that C was the Roman numeral for 100 (that's easy to remember because *C* starts the word "century," which is 100 years). I traced 100 in the dust beneath the letter *C*.

"And L is the Roman numeral for 50," said Lamar, "which means LI = 50 + 1, or 51."

He completed our list. We had now translated the Roman numerals in Zell's message to the numbers:

4, 1, 5, 100, 51, 9

"I'll bet you 10 to 1 that this is the combination to open the vault," I said.

"That's one bet I'm *not* going to take," said Lamar, "because I think you're right."

He turned the six dials to the corresponding numbers, and I pulled on the handle again. This time the door swung open easily, revealing a deep, black six-sided hole. A wave of cold air rushed out, but it was too dark to see what was inside.

"Cross your fingers," said Lamar. "Let's hope Zell left us something good."

He stuck his hand into the vault.

I held my breath for what seemed like an eternity (though in reality, it was only seventeen seconds). With a scraping sound, Lamar slid something out of the vault and set it down on one of the shelves. It was a metal box the size of two math books stacked together. Engraved on the top

of the box was the Zanarian seal: three concentric circles and a Z.

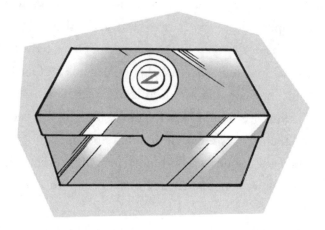

Lamar lifted the hinged lid.

The box was filled with devices made out of black wire. They looked like headsets for listening to music, with tiny twelve-sided blocks attached to each end (dodecahedrons, to be precise).

We each lifted one out.

"Ready to give them a try?" asked Lamar.

"Definitely," I said.

We both slid one onto our heads with the tiny blocks tucked inside our ears.

"Notice anything different?"

All I noticed was a faint buzzing sound, as if two lazy mosquitoes were trapped inside my brain.

"It would help if we had an instruction manual," I said.

Lamar searched inside the vault, and I checked all six

faces on the metal box looking for more inscriptions, but we both came up empty-handed.

"We know Zell wanted us to use these things to talk with the penguins," said Lamar, "but so far that baby penguin has been the only one we've seen. There have to be more penguins someplace else that we can talk to. One baby penguin alone couldn't invade an entire planet. "

"I think we should look for their spaceship," I said. "If we find their spaceship, we'll find more penguins."

"And the sooner we find more penguins," said Lamar, "the sooner we can stop them from turning the Zanarians to stone."

Fooz had said that the penguins' spaceship was outside of the city, but so far we had only been looking *inside* the buildings. The door leading outside from this room was locked. No matter how we searched, neither of us could find a keyhole or a lock or a secret lever that would let us open it.

Did that mean we were stuck?

Absolutely not.

The map on the back of the transport cube showed us the way to get outside.

I had noticed that there were four points on the map that *weren't* touching any of the buildings. It made sense that these spots would take us outside. But which one to try?

The point on the map that I wanted to try was beneath a rectangle and between two buildings the same area in size. Lamar, however, wanted to try the point that was between a symmetrical pentagon and an asymmetrical heptagon.

Even though we had been in agreement all day, I could

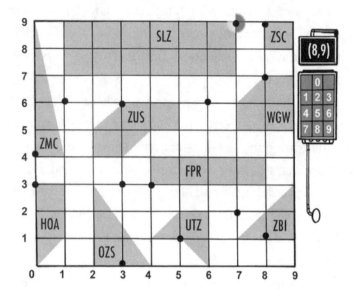

tell we were heading toward an argument. Lamar can be pretty stubborn. In fact, he can be as stubborn as . . . well, as stubborn as I am. So instead of arguing, we decided to ask Abe.

Abe was Lamar's lucky penny. We sometimes asked for his help when we had two equal choices, such as which of us got to go first when playing a computer game. Lamar flipped Abe into the air. I called

"Tails!" and Abe landed in Lamar's palm. He slapped the coin onto the back of his arm. "Sorry, Lexie," he said, showing me the penny. "It's heads." Then he punched the coordinates (6, 6) into the transport cube's keypad.

When we crawled out of the transport cube this time, we *were* outside. Over our heads a quartet of orange suns shone down on us. Their bright rays reflected off the surrounding metal buildings, making them shine with an

orange glow. In fact, everything seemed to be made of metal: the buildings, the street, the transport cube. The only things that *weren't* made out of metal were the black-and-white penguins.

And there were penguins everywhere! Not baby penguins like we had seen in the Zanarian Security Chamber, but adult penguins as tall as our shoulders. From where I was standing, I quickly counted five more than two dozen. They were waddling up and down the street in all directions, swiveling their heads from side to side and squawking, "Awk? Awk? Awk?" The air smelled like someone had just opened a ten-ton can of sardines.

The poor Zanarians! How could they stand a chance against a flock of penguins this big?

One of the penguins waddled over to us and turned its head sideways. "Awk?" it asked.

Here was our chance to try the communicators.

"Hello there," I replied. "My name is Lexie, and this is Lamar and we're hoping you can—"

That's all I got out before the penguin squawked, "Awk! Awk! Awk!" and waddled away.

"I don't know about you, but all I got was a lot of static," said Lamar. "How much of that did you understand?"

"Not even one percent," I replied. "Maybe the penguins have to be wearing one of the headsets, too."

But getting one of the penguins to wear a headset proved as tricky as nailing down a repeating decimal.

When Lamar walked up to a penguin to try to slip a communicator over its head, the penguin squawked angrily,

chased him, then nipped Lamar on the back of his leg.

"Ouch!" he yelped. "Cut it out!" But the penguin was already gone.

Lamar rubbed his calf. "There has to be a less painful way to get one of these devices on a penguin."

We walked down the street between the metallic buildings, passing even more noisy penguins on our left and right as the fish smell grew stronger. Then, when we turned a corner, we saw it.

In a large open area at the edge of the buildings towered a spaceship eleven times larger than Fooz's. It was shaped like the lower half of a sphere and topped by a tall cone. The entire thing was bright blue and reminded me of a giant raindrop or an overturned single-scoop blueberry ice-cream cone. At its base, on long ramps set at thirty-degree angles,

agitated penguins waddled in and out. The sound of their honking and squawking was louder than a 5:00 p.m. traffic jam, and the fish smell was almost more than I could stand.

In front of the ship on a raised platform was a penguin slightly larger than the rest. He was definitely making the most noise. He squawked and pointed his flipper, and then several penguins ran off in that direction. He squawked again and pointed in the opposite direction, and more penguins waddled away.

"*That's* the penguin we want to talk to," said Lamar. "And I think I know how we can do it. If you can keep him distracted, Lexie, I'll sneak up behind him and drop a communicator over his head before he even realizes I'm there."

I cautiously approached the penguin-in-charge, holding my nose so I wouldn't faint from the smell. When I was ten feet in front of him, I waved my hand.

"Excuse me, Mr. Penguin . . . but could I have a minute, or two, or three of your time?"

The penguin looked at me and squawked, "Awk! Awk! Awk!" The static in my ears ratcheted up several decibels, and the nearby penguins looked at me suspiciously.

Meanwhile I saw Lamar sneaking up behind the bird, holding an extra headset in his hands. I needed to make sure this penguin didn't turn around, so I continued talking, even if he couldn't understand me.

"You look upset," I told the penguin. "I know that feeling. And do you know what I do when I'm upset and want to calm down? I count. Maybe you should try counting, too. You might feel better. As a matter of fact, that's just what I've

43

been doing now. I've been counting penguins. And do you know how many I've counted? I've reached a three-digit even number that reads the same backward as forward. It's more than twenty times my age, but less than thirty times my age, and if you add the digits together, they total 8. Since I'm eleven years old, that means that I've counted . . ."

A few penguins had gathered around me. They were as agitated as their leader.

"AWK!" they squawked. "AWK! AWK! AWK!"

The penguins looked mad, their beaks looked sharp, and I was getting nervous. Fortunately Lamar was within striking range. He reached up and dropped a communicator over the penguin's ears . . . or at least where you'd guess a penguin's ears would be.

Instantly the crackling static cleared up, and through the headset came a voice that sounded like a very angry duck.

". . . and if you don't bring her back NOW," shouted the penguin, "this means WAR!"

CHAPTER 五

Penguin Pandemonium

"**H**old on!" I said. "We don't want to start a war!" Especially not with 242 (or more) penguins.

"Aha! At last you are speaking a language that I understand!" said the penguin. He didn't seem to notice that Lamar had slipped a communicator over his head. "If you don't want a war, then return my precious Ping to me immediately!" He stomped one of his webbed feet for emphasis and almost tipped over in the process.

"Who is Ping?" I said.

"And not to be rude, but who are *you*?" added Lamar, who was now standing beside me.

The penguin straightened to his full height, which I estimated to be about one yard, one foot, and one inch tall. He lifted his beak high into the air.

"I am King Pong, supreme ruler of Planet Pengolia.

The crew of my spaceship and I are mapping the far reaches of our galaxy. And Ping is my daughter, the royal princess. We landed on your planet to replenish our water supply, and my darling Ping, being the curious creature that she is, wandered off to explore. That's when she was kidnapped! Now, bring her back at once, or face the mighty wrath of Pengolia!"

All the penguins within a thirty-foot radius began flapping their flippers against their sides and squawking wildly.

"Take it easy!" said Lamar. "How do you know your daughter's been kidnapped?"

"Of course she's been kidnapped! She promised she would be back by now and she's not! Why else would she be gone so long? Now return her at once!"

The Zanarians were so afraid of penguins I knew they'd never try to kidnap the princess, not in a dozen decades. But an idea was beginning to form in my brain.

"Is your daughter about so tall?" I asked, spreading my hands ten inches apart. "And covered with fluff?"

"Yes!" said King Pong, "And she is brave and beautiful and smarter than ninety percent of the other penguins on my planet, even though she is still a young chick. Bring her back now, or your planet will suffer the consequences!"

The circle of penguins around us hopped up and down angrily.

"First of all, this is *not* our planet," said Lamar, "and second of all, she has *not* been kidnapped."

"If she has not been kidnapped, then what have you done with her?"

"We haven't done anything with her," I said. "She's only wandering around inside these buildings."

She's also turning the entire city's population into statues, I thought.

"Storm the buildings!" shouted King Pong. "Break down the doors! Drill through the walls! We must rescue the royal princess!"

The penguins went crazy. They frantically waddled into the spaceship, then poured out again, holding ten-foot-long poles with diamond-shaped tips under their wings.

"What a bunch of loony birds!" said Lamar. "If they're not careful, they're going to hurt someone."

"And if they get inside the buildings, any of the Zanarians who *haven't* been turned to stone yet won't stand a chance," I said.

The penguins waddled toward the nearest building, waving their poles and throwing rocks from pouches they had slung around their necks. One of the rocks ricocheted off a wall, bounced off the metallic road, and sailed past our heads, nearly nailing my left ear.

"Stop it!" shouted Lamar. "Put away your weapons! You don't have to destroy anything! Lexie and I will bring back your daughter."

King Pong made a shrill whistle from the back of his throat. The crazy penguins came to a sudden halt, sending three-fifths of them tumbling into a huge heap.

"You will return my precious Ping?" asked the king.

"Yes," said Lamar. "We'll bring her back . . . as long as you promise to leave this planet in peace."

"Gladly," said Pong. "Return Princess Ping within one Chronok, and we'll be happy to leave this planet."

"A Chronok?" I asked. "How long is that?"

"Guards, show them!"

One of the taller penguins waddled up and handed us a round, flat object that resembled a hiking compass. The circular face of the Chronok was divided into nine equal wedges, like slices on a pizza. A single blue arrow, like the minute hand of a clock, extended from the center of the circle.

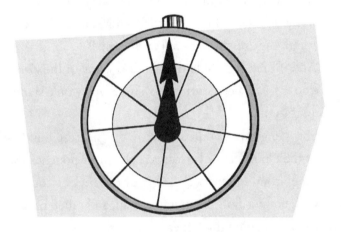

Pong tapped a small button at the top of the Chronok, and it began to vibrate in my palm.

"When the blue arrow makes a complete revolution around the dial, that will be one Chronok," he said. "And if the princess is not back by then, we attack!"

"No problem," said Lamar. "She'll be back. Just keep your army from going ballistic and tearing down these buildings."

We hurried away from the spaceship toward the transport cube. When we were out of earshot of the king, I asked, "So, where do we find Ping?"

"Beats me," said Lamar. "But we're smart, Lexie. I have no doubt the two of us can figure it out."

We ducked inside the transport cube to think. The penguins that were still roaming the streets ignored us. By this time, the arrow on the Chronok had already traveled across one of the nine wedges, turning it blue. That left eight wedges to go. According to my watch, it had taken five minutes for the arrow to cover one wedge. I worked out the math in my head.

"We don't have a lot of time," I said. "Only forty minutes."

Lamar nodded at the map.

"There are ten buildings to search," he said. "So that gives us just four minutes to search each building."

"We could split up," I suggested, "but that still gives us only eight minutes per building. Can we can narrow our search?"

"Good idea," said Lamar. "Let's start by reviewing what we already know."

That's always a wise strategy when trying to solve a problem.

"We know that the princess isn't very big, but that she's very smart . . . at least smarter than the other penguins," said Lamar.

"And we know that she's already visited at least two of the buildings," I said, "The room filled with spaceships, SLZ, and the Zanarian Security Chamber, ZSC."

49

"And we also know that she didn't return to her father when she said she would," said Lamar.

"But we don't know *why* she didn't return," I added.

"Maybe she's just being curious, like her father told us," said Lamar. "Or maybe she wants to run away from her crazy dad and she's searching the city for a place to hide."

Lamar and I tried running away from home once when we were only preschoolers. We were going to live on the roof of our apartment building, but we couldn't reach the elevator button to take us all the way to the roof. We ended up building a fort in his bunk beds instead.

Picturing us as preschoolers in the elevator triggered something in my brain. It reminded me of seeing the princess escaping in the transport cube. Something about the two scenes was similar.

"How about this for a plan," said Lamar. "Let's start by searching the smallest buildings first. We can search them the fastest. We've already been to the Zanarian Security Chamber, so let's start by searching buildings UTZ and ZBI. They're the next smallest buildings in size."

While Lamar checked the coordinates on the map, I was still picturing Ping in the transport cube, reaching for the keypad. Something about that image kept nagging at me. Suddenly, a 500-watt lightbulb went on in my brain.

"No!" I exclaimed. "Ping can't be in any of those buildings!"

Lamar looked surprised.

"Why not?"

"Look at the coordinates for the two buildings where

we've already seen Ping," I said. "And then compare them to the keypad. What do you notice?"

Lamar studied the grid.

"Well . . . the coordinates for the transport cube in the spaceship room are (7, 8). The coordinates for the transport cube in the Zanarian Security Council are (8, 9). And 7, 8, and 9 are the last three numbers on the bottom of the keypad."

"Exactly!" I said. "Don't you get it?"

Lamar shook his head.

"Those are the only numbers Ping can reach!" I said. "Remember how she had to stretch to reach even the bottom row of numbers on the keypad? She's too small to reach the numbers higher up!"

The lightbulb went on in Lamar's brain, too.

"And that's why she never returned to her father's spaceship," he said. "She couldn't reach the coordinates that would take her back to one of the outdoor cubes!"

If Ping could only reach the numbers 7, 8, and 9 on the

keypad, that definitely limited the number of buildings she could visit. In fact, there were only nine different coordinate pairs she could make with those numbers. And only three of those pairs matched up with dots on the map. We knew she had already visited two of those spots, so . . .

Lamar and I were in agreement. Assuming she hadn't backtracked, we knew which building we should search first.

"And we'd better search it fast," I said. "There's only two-thirds of the Chronok left."

That was thirty minutes.

I looked at the building where we were headed.

WGW.

Wiggling Garden Worms?

Weird Green Warthogs?

Western Groundhog Washroom?

I wondered what the letters stood for.

Lamar entered the coordinates (8, 7) into the keypad.

"WGW," he said, "here we come!"

CHAPTER 75% OF 8

A Watery Dilemma

When we crawled out of the transport cube, the light around us shimmered and rippled like sunlight at the bottom of a nine-foot swimming pool. The air was cool and moist on my arms. I thought I heard the soft lapping sound of waves.

But we weren't underwater. We were in a room filled with transparent boxes. Each box was the size of a large school backpack. Inside the boxes we could see round spheres that looked like pale-blue water balloons. It was the spheres that were giving off the watery glow.

"I don't see Ping," said Lamar, sniffing the air, "but I can sure smell her."

He was right. The room definitely smelled fishy. We were on the right track.

"You go left, and I'll go right," he said. "We'll search the room faster that way."

The transparent boxes were stacked three feet over my head. They formed twisting, narrow aisles that made me feel as if I was swimming through an underwater maze.

I knew that if we didn't find Ping soon we'd be in trouble. The whole planet would be in trouble. And because I was worried, I started doing what I always do. I counted.

The obvious things to count were the stacks of boxes that made up the walls on either side of me. I had counted forty-four stacks on my right and forty-six stacks on my left when I turned a corner and almost tripped over something small, gray, and fluffy. It was the royal princess. She was trying to push one of the transparent boxes along the floor.

When she saw me, her tiny black eyes doubled in size until they were as big as nickels. She waddled away from me as fast as she could, but she only took eleven steps before she bumped into Lamar, who was coming from the opposite direction.

Trapped between us, she climbed up onto the box she had been trying to push. Then she glared defiantly at us.

"Getting a headset on her is going to be tricky," said Lamar. "She's not going to let us sneak up on her like we did with her dad. Maybe I could just grab her, and then you could drop a communicator over her head."

I shook my head.

"She might be small," I said, "but look at that beak. It's as sharp as a number-two pencil before a test. Besides, she's just a baby penguin. We don't want to scare her."

"PEEP!" shouted the princess. "PEEP! PEEP! PEEP!"

"Hmmm," said Lamar. "I've had my share of dealing

with little kids. Remember last week when we were baby-sitting my little brother and he wouldn't put on his shoes so we could take him to the park? We tricked him into wearing his shoes by pretending we *didn't* want him to wear them. Maybe the same thing would work with the princess."

It was a good idea.

I opened the box of communicators I had been carrying under my arm. I chose the smallest headset and held it close to my chest as if I didn't want Ping to see it. I motioned for Lamar to come closer. We huddled around the headset together and laughed as if we were having the best time in the world.

When I took a quick glance over my shoulder, I saw that our plan was working. Ping was watching us closely. She slowly climbed down from the box and waddled toward us. We pretended not to notice. Fortunately, she was as curious as her father had said. A few seconds later, Ping pushed

her little head between our ankles and looked up to see what we were doing.

I held the headset up higher so she couldn't reach it and shook my head no. Ping began jumping for it. Even without the communicator, I could almost hear her saying, "Gimmee! Gimmee! Gimmee! Gimmee!"

I gave a pretend sigh and lowered it onto her head. Instantly her squeaky voice came through the earpieces.

"What is this thing? Who are you? Why do you keep following me? And if you try to hurt me, you great big monsters, I'll bite your funny-looking feet!" She then began pecking at my tennis shoes with her tiny sharp beak.

"Take it easy," said Lamar. "We're not going to hurt you. We only want to take you back to your father."

She looked at us skeptically and put her stubby little flippers on her fuzzy hips.

"I don't believe you." Then she grabbed Lamar's shoelace and began pulling.

"It's true," I said. "Look."

I held out the Chronok that King Pong had given us. By now, five of the nine wedges had turned blue.

"Your father gave us this when he sent us to find you. He's worried because you didn't return to your spaceship when you said you would."

Princess Ping dropped Lamar's shoelace from her beak.

"I couldn't return!" she squawked. "I couldn't reach the right buttons!"

My theory was correct!

"And now I was trying to push one of these boxes over to the keypad so I could reach the numbers to take me back," said Ping. "But the box is too heavy."

"Then it's a good thing we came along," said Lamar, retying his shoe. "Come with us, and we'll take you to your dad right now."

You would have thought that Lamar had said he was

going to drop three six-pack crates of fifteen-pound bowling balls on top of the princess.

"NO!" she squawked. "No! No! No!"

She threw herself down onto the floor and began kicking her tiny feet. "I'm not going anywhere without these boxes!"

"But you don't need them," I said. "We can push the buttons for you."

"I need what's *inside* the boxes," demanded Ping. "When we landed on this planet, we wanted to refill our water supply. I decided to find the water all by myself. And I did! I found a whole room full of water globes, just like we have on our planet."

So that's what WGW stood for: Water Globe Warehouse!

"And I'm going to bring them all back to my daddy, or I won't leave!" she pouted. "So there!"

The princess might be smart and curious, but she was also as spoiled as last year's yogurt.

I thought about the size of the transport cube and compared that to the size of these boxes. At most, we could fit ten boxes in at once. I had already counted ninety stacks. There were nine boxes in each stack. To transport just the boxes I had counted would require . . . eighty-one trips!

"You don't need them *all*?" I asked. "Do you?"

"Noooooo," said Princess Ping reluctantly. "I suppose not. Water globes are concentrated. That means that one little globe makes a *lot* of water. We only need one globe for every twenty penguins on our ship."

The spaceship was huge. I had counted 242 penguins earlier, but I knew there must be more than that. A LOT more. Maybe even triple that amount.

"Just how many penguins *are* on your ship?" asked Lamar.

Ping puckered her forehead in concentration.

"I don't know for sure," she said. "But Daddy told me that one-fourth of the penguins on the spaceship come from the southern hemisphere of our planet."

Lamar took out his pocket notebook and jotted that down.

"And one-third of *those* penguins live in our capital city, where I live."

Lamar jotted that down, too.

"And one-half of *those* penguins belong to the royal family, like me."

I looked at what Lamar had written down so far. It still wasn't enough information for us to figure out the total number of penguins on her spaceship.

"Do you know how many penguins on your ship belong to the royal family?" I asked.

"Of course I do," said Ping. "There's me and my daddy and my thirty-three cousins."

Lamar jotted that down. Yes! We finally had all we needed to know.

"If we bring back enough water for all the penguins on your ship," said Lamar, "will you go with us back to your father?"

Ping scrunched up her face as she made up her mind.

"Okay," she said. "As long as you tell Daddy that *I'm* the one who found all the water globes."

I checked the Chronok. Only a third of the wedges remained. That was fifteen minutes. I hoped that was enough time for us to calculate the number of penguins on the spaceship . . . and figure out the amount of water globes we needed . . . and get Ping back to Pong.

If not, we'd be smack in the middle of an intergalactic penguin war.

CHAPTER (22 ÷ 2) - (2 × 2)

What's Smoo?

Figuring out how many penguins were on Ping's spaceship seemed complicated, but Lamar and I have had lots of practice solving complicated challenges at our math tournaments. And in fact, this problem wasn't so complicated after all. Not when we worked it backward, one step at a time.

To start, we knew how many penguins on the ship were from the royal family: thirty-five—Pong, Ping, and her thirty-three cousins.

Thirty-five was one-half the number of penguins from the capital city, so the total number would be *two* halves, or 2 × 35, which is 70.

Seventy was one-third of the penguins from the southern hemisphere of Pengolia, so the total number of penguins from the southern hemisphere would be *three* thirds, or 3 × 70, which is 210.

And 210 was one-fourth of the penguins on the ship, so the total number of penguins on the ship would be *four fourths*, or 4 × 210, which is 840.

"If there are 840 penguins on your ship," Lamar told Ping, "and you need one water globe for every twenty penguins, then we need to bring back . . ."

"Forty-two water globes," Lamar and I said at the same time.

Ping flapped her fuzzy wings and did a little happy dance.

"My daddy is going to be so proud of me!"

Lamar leaned down to pick up the box that Ping had been trying to push across the floor.

"*Ooof!*" he grunted. "That's heavy! I hope we don't have to carry many of these. How many globes are in each of these boxes?"

I examined the boxes and noticed that each one was labeled with a tiny tag in the corner indicating how many globes were inside. But even though the boxes were the same size, they held different numbers of water globes. There were six different numbers of water globes that the boxes contained:

13 water globes

14 water globes

19 water globes

22 water globes

23 water globes

or

27 water globes

We wanted enough water for all the penguins, but if the boxes were as heavy as Lamar said, we didn't want to carry more water globes than we needed.

Fortunately there was a combination of two boxes that totaled exactly the amount of globes we wanted: forty-two. If Lamar and I each took a box, we could bring back enough water to the spaceship in just one trip.

I checked the Chronok. There was only one wedge left before our time expired.

"If we don't want King Pong to destroy all the buildings in the city, we had better get going *now*," I said. I picked up one of the boxes after placing the metal container with the communicators on top.

Oof! Lamar was right! These boxes *were* heavy! Mine must have weighed twice as much as our weekly recycling bin.

Lamar and I quickly hurried down the narrow aisles with our boxes to the transport cube, but once we got there, we had to wait for Ping to catch up with us. When she did, she squawked, "I want to push the buttons! Let me do it!"

Lamar set his box on the floor of the cube and then lifted Ping on top of the box. She reached up with a feathered flipper and slapped it twice against the number 6. Just like that, we were outside again. But now the streets of Naznar were empty. There wasn't another penguin in sight. Not a good sign.

The Chronok in my pocket began to buzz. I didn't have to check to know what that meant. Our time was up, and King Pong was assembling his army and getting ready to attack.

Lamar picked up his box again, with Ping riding on top. "C'mon, Lexie!" he called. "Run!"

If it had been track-and-field day, I bet we would have set a record for the fifty-yard dash.

Then, when we turned the corner, I almost dropped the box I was carrying. The spaceship was still there, and King Pong was still standing on his platform, but now he was surrounded by the entire crew from his ship. If you've never seen 839 penguins gathered together at once, it's overwhelming, not to mention horrifically smelly.

But what really started my heart thumping was that all of these penguins were waving sticks or spears or other sharp and pointed nasty-looking weapons.

"The enemy has not returned!" shouted Pong. "And the princess is still missing. And that can mean only one thing!"

The mob of penguins stomped their weapons on the metal street. My ears rang with the clatter of a thousand angry alarm clocks.

"That's right!" continued Pong. "That means WAR! When I give the signal, charge the buildings! Storm the structures! Don't leave a single wall standing until the princess is returned!"

The penguins were going berserk! We were too late!

"BUT I'M RIGHT HERE!" shouted Ping at the top

64

of her tiny little lungs. Who knew one small bird could be so loud?

All 1,678 penguin eyes turned in our direction. Ping jumped up and down on the box Lamar was carrying and waved her flippers.

"My baby!" called Pong. He leapt off his platform and ran toward us, scattering penguins as he came. He grabbed Ping in his flippers and lifted her up, then nuzzled her with his beak.

"I thought I had lost you forever," he cooed.

Ping wiggled out from his grip. "Look at what I brought back, Daddy. I brought back water for everyone on our ship!"

I set my box on the ground and opened the lid. King Pong peered inside at the water globes.

"There are nineteen globes in this box, and in that box there are twenty-three," peeped Ping.

"My goodness!" said Pong. "I always knew Daddy's perfect precious penguin was the smartest penguin in the entire galaxy!"

Lamar rolled his eyes. Who knew penguins could be so gushy?

We cleared our throats, and the king finally noticed us.

"Thank you for returning my daughter," he said. "I am indebted to both of you. And never let it be said that King Pong is not true to his word. My subjects and I will leave this planet at once."

He turned to the sea of black-and-white birds watching us.

"Penguins of Pengolia! The brilliant and beloved princess has returned, triumphant in her search for water! We can return to our spaceship peacefully and continue on our journey!"

The penguins gave three happy squawks. Then they turned and began scurrying up the long ramps that led into their ship.

"Before you go," I said to the king, "we have a favor to ask, and it's important. Our friends who live on this planet were turned to stone when they saw you. Do you know how we can turn them back?"

King Pong stroked his chin. "Turned to stone? How very odd. I have been ruler of Pengolia for over 233,000 Chronoks and I have never heard of that happening before. But because you have returned my daughter, I will give the matter my deepest consideration."

He closed his eyes.

Five seconds later, he opened them.

"After much thought I can say with 100 percent certainty that I have no idea how to turn your friends back. But if I ever think of a way to help you, I will be sure to come back and let you know. Good luck, and good-bye."

Then he turned and waddled toward the ship.

Was that it? Would Fooz and the other Zanarians stay stone statues forever? No! There *had* to be a way to save them.

Princess Ping chased after her father.

"Wait, Daddy! Give them some Smoo! Give them some now!"

Smoo?

"Of course," said the king. "You are a genius!" He flapped his flippers three times and called, "Bring me a bag of Smoo at once!"

Faster than you can round 99 to the nearest hundred, another penguin arrived dragging a large cloth sack. King Pong presented the heavy gray sack to us.

"Inside you will find our planet's strongest medicine, a light-green liquid called Smoo. Mix precisely one Veng of Smoo with one of the small pellets that you will also find in the bag. You will have a powerful antidote for almost any disease. I don't know if it will work on creatures that have been turned to stone, but it is the best that I can offer."

"But how much is a Veng?" I said.

King Pong shook his head. "What strange creatures you are. You don't know how long a Chronok is, and you don't know how much a Veng is. But do not worry. There is

a complete set of measuring containers in the bag. You will have no difficulty measuring the amount that you need."

"Thank you," said Lamar. "And our friends thank you, too."

By now only Ping, Pong, and a handful of other penguins remained on the ground; the rest had boarded the ship. Ping and her father turned to leave, but I said, "One more thing."

I reached into my pocket and handed Pong the Chronok that he had given us.

"And I need to return these communicators back to the Zanarians."

I carefully lifted them off their heads.

Ping looked up at us and waved her flipper. She said something, but now it only sounded like "Awk! Awk! Awk!"

Lamar and I waved back.

When all the penguins had boarded the ship, the ramps retracted and the doors closed. Without a sound, the giant teardrop began to spin like a top, slowly at first, then faster. It lifted three feet off the ground, then six feet, then twelve feet. When it reached twenty-four feet . . .

Whoosh!

It shot straight up into the sky and was gone.

"Good luck to the inhabitants of the next planet they visit," Lamar said. "Now let's go help Fooz!"

I shook my head no.

"We can't."

Lamar raised his eyebrows.

"What are you talking about?"

I had been checking inside the bag.

"Here's the Smoo," I said, holding up a large jug of green liquid. It was as big as a quart of cider and so cold that the outside of the container was frosty. "And here's the jar of pellets." They looked like crystal-clear pickles, the baby dill size. "But there's a hole in the bottom of the bag. The measuring containers are missing. Without them, we can't mix the cure for Fooz, and we can't bring her back to life."

CHAPTER 2048 ... 512 ... 128 ... 32 ...?

Deep-Fried Faznan

Lamar and I searched the entire area where the penguins' spaceship had landed, square foot by square foot. We found two broken spears, three piles of fish bones, and enough black-and-white feathers to stuff a four-cushioned sofa and a king-size recliner. We also found two measuring containers, one labeled *8 Vengs* and one labeled *5 Vengs*.

We did *not* find the measuring container labeled *1 Veng*.

"It must have fallen out when the bag was still inside the ship," I said. That meant it was now on its way to another planet ... or perhaps to another galaxy.

"Maybe we don't need it," said Lamar. "Now that the penguins are gone, maybe Fooz is back to her old self."

I was skeptical, but it was worth checking. Sometimes even unlikely solutions can be correct. We took the transport

cube back to the coordinates (7, 8), but the frightened group of Zanarians at the far end of the building were still statues. And when we climbed the ramp into Fooz's spaceship, she was standing in the exact position we had left her, solid as a block of granite.

"We came back," I told Fooz, "just as we promised."

"And we've got the antidote," said Lamar. "At least, we *hope* we've got the antidote."

But we still didn't know how to measure the correct amount.

"Maybe we can find the right measuring container in Fooz's ship," I suggested.

We searched the ship from the fuel bay below to the engine compartment overhead. We found lots of oddly shaped gadgets, including a three-pronged screwdriver, a circular ruler, and a pair of scissors only four centimeters long. But we didn't find anything resembling a measuring container in *any* size.

"I've been thinking," said Lamar. "Maybe we don't need a one-Veng measuring cup after all."

"But you heard what Pong said," I told him. "We need to measure *exactly* one Veng of Smoo for the antidote."

"True," said Lamar. "But maybe we can use the five- and eight-Veng containers to measure that amount."

He had a good point. With just those two containers, it was possible to measure different amounts. For example, if we filled the eight-Veng container then poured it into the five-Veng container, we'd have exactly 3 Vengs of Smoo left over.

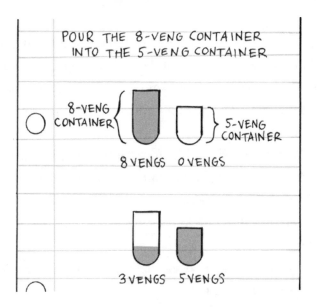

POUR THE 8-VENG CONTAINER
INTO THE 5-VENG CONTAINER

8-VENG CONTAINER

5-VENG CONTAINER

8 VENGS   0 VENGS

3 VENGS   5 VENGS

But was it possible to measure just *one* Veng of Smoo with the two containers we had?

We'd never know unless we tried.

Being careful not to spill a drop, we began pouring the cold, thick green liquid from one container to the other and sometimes back into the original bottle. I carefully took notes on a scrap of paper so that we always knew exactly how much was in each container.

It was tricky. Sometimes we had to start over. But with Fooz's stone body watching us, we had good motivation to keep trying. Persistence paid off.

After a lot of trial and error, we ended up with exactly one Veng of Smoo in the eight-Veng container.

"Now all we need is the antidote pill."

I unscrewed the lid from the jar and dropped one pickle-shaped pellet into the green liquid. Instantly it began to fizz like a freshly poured glass of soda. It also changed

color, from green to pink to yellow to blue. A thin white mist floated up from the container, smelling like a mango-strawberry smoothie. That left us with a new challenge.

"How do we get Fooz to drink this?" said Lamar. "I could tilt her body backward. Then we could pour the liquid down her throat."

"Or maybe we're supposed to pour the mixture right on top of her," I said.

"No, no! Please do not pour anything on top of me," said a familiar high-pitched voice.

It was Fooz!

"You can talk!" Lamar and I shouted.

Not only could she talk, but she could move again, too. One by one she stretched each of her six legs.

"Yes, yes. I can talk." She leaned toward the bubbling liquid and took a deep whiff. "What is that delicious smell? It makes my entire body tingle." She inhaled again, and the color began creeping its way back across her shaggy body, one inch at a time.

"I feel as if I have missed out on something," Fooz said. "The last thing I remember was bringing the two of you aboard my spaceship and asking for your help. And now . . ." She peered out the spaceship door and down the ramp. "I see that we are already back on Zan. How did we get here?"

Lamar and I explained everything that had happened since Fooz had turned to stone. Her antenna eyes grew especially wide when we explained the bubbling mixture. I showed her my notes on how we had measured exactly one Veng of Smoo.

"Excellent, excellent!" exclaimed Fooz. "And all of the penguins have departed? Then we must bring this wonderfully aromatic antidote to the other Zanarians at once!"

We carried the bubbling liquid to the statues at the other end of the spaceship garage. When they got a whiff of the mixture, the life slowly crept up through their bodies, just as it had with Fooz. Fooz recognized them as members of the security council. They had been hoping to meet us when we landed, but unfortunately for them, they ran into Ping first.

The members of the council followed us back to the security chamber. When we arrived, the mixture in the eight-Veng container was still bubbling enough to restore the Zanarian who was hiding under the table. And it wasn't just any Zanarian, it was Zell, the council's leader.

After telling all of them our story, Zell bowed to us and proclaimed, "You are national heroes. How can we ever repay you?"

"We must have a celebration!" said another member of the council.

"Yes, yes," said a third member. "A celebration with music and plenty of deep-fried Faznan!"

We looked at Fooz.

"What is Faznan?"

"That is our planet's most prized delicacy," said Fooz. "You should be honored. We eat it only on the most special of occasions. I believe you have something similar on your planet: electric eels." She licked her long blue tongue across the front of her sharp pointed teeth.

Lamar and I grimaced at each other.

"Gee, thanks, Zell," said Lamar. "That sounds delicious, but I think we need to head home. We have to study for a spelling test."

Even studying for a spelling test sounded better than eating electric eels.

We handed her the bag from the penguins, making sure to point out the hole at the bottom. Then I explained my notes on how to measure one Veng of Smoo. The mixture we had made was no longer bubbling, but there was still plenty of the creamy green liquid left in the bottle and a whole jar of the pellets.

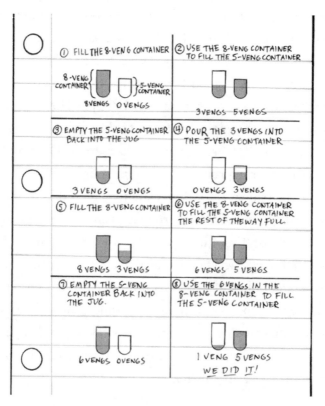

"You'll be ready in case any of those penguins ever come back," I said.

Zell immediately sent the other members of the security council off to locate any other Zanarians who might have been turned to stone. She then escorted us back to Fooz's spaceship.

When we arrived at the spaceship garage, a large party of Zanarians had already gathered to see us off. I couldn't help it; I counted them. Not including Fooz, the number of Zanarians was one-fourteenth the number of penguins from Pengolia.

"We will remember you forever," said Zell. "We will erect a statue of the two of you in the spot where the Pengolian spaceship landed. It will remind us of the Earthlings who saved us from becoming statues ourselves."

After saying good-bye to the sixty Zanarians, we climbed aboard the spaceship and strapped ourselves in. Fooz started the engine. Before I could finish counting the number of bolts that secured our chairs to the floor, we had blasted off through an opening in the roof.

Fooz's ship was fast, but it still took us a while to return to Earth: 4 and 5/9ths Chronoks, using Pengolian time. From our last trip with her, we knew that Fooz could return us back home at whatever time we wanted. We chose to arrive home only forty-five seconds after we had left. That way we wouldn't get in trouble for being gone so long, and our families wouldn't be worried about what had happened to us. Penguin fathers aren't the only parents who go crazy when their kids are missing.

"I am very proud of you," said Fooz as she prepared to beam us back to Earth. "I was confident that the two of you could save our planet."

She held out a metal box. "Zell insisted that you have this."

I took the box, and Lamar said, "It was great seeing you, Fooz."

"I hope our paths cross again," I added, "sometime when there aren't any penguins around."

"That is what I hope also," said Fooz.

She entered three numbers into her control panel, and before we knew it, Lamar and I were sitting at my kitchen table.

"Wow, that was a lot more interesting than studying spelling words," I said.

"Yes, that predicament had undeniable appeal," said Lamar. *Predicament*, *undeniable*, and *appeal* were all spelling words. "Now let's see what's in the box that Zell gave us."

The box was engraved with the Zanarian seal and looked exactly like the one we had found inside the vault.

"Maybe it's the . . ."

"Translators!" finished Lamar. "Excellent! If those headsets allowed us to talk to penguins, maybe we can talk to the animals on our planet, too."

Talking with dogs and cats and even squirrels in the park . . . the possibilities were infinite. Maybe I could fit a headset onto one of my goldfish. I've always wondered what they thought about during the day.

I lifted the lid and inside the metal box were . . . eight

charred black sticks that looked like foot-long mummified earthworms. Not only did they look disgusting, but they also smelled like cottage cheese three months past its expiration date.

"Deep-fried Faznan," groaned Lamar.

I closed the lid.

"Here's a new math problem for you," I said. "If you take two smart kids and add one box of deep-fried Faznan, how many stomachaches will you get?"

"That's the easiest math problem we've solved all day," said Lamar. "The answer is zero. The kids are too smart to eat anything that disgusting."

"I wholeheartedly concur," I told him. *Concur* was the last of our spelling words. "Instead, let's each have a brownie. We earned them. And this time, I bet I'll finish my brownie even before you!"

LAMAR'S NOTEBOOK

Hey! This is Lamar. And this is my private notebook. (Don't worry, I don't mind if you're reading it.) I use it to keep track of the strange adventures that happen to Lexie and me—especially the math-related parts of our adventures. Someday, when I'm a famous mathematician giving lectures around the world (and maybe even across the galaxy), I want to be able to remember all the things that happened to me as a kid. For example, the time Lexie and I saved an entire planet using math. Not too many kids get to save an entire planet when they're only eleven years old.

I also use my notebook to make up math puzzles to stump Lexie and the other kids on our Math All-Stars team. Maybe I'll be able to stump you, too!

On the Grid

Fooz's planet of Zan was pretty interesting: a city made of metal, a sky with four suns, a giant parking lot for spaceships. But the best part was the transport cubes. I'd love to build some of those cubes here on Earth. I'd never have to ride the school bus again! That would save me twenty minutes each morning and twenty minutes each afternoon. Since there are 180 days of school each year, I'd end up with an extra 120 *hours* to do whatever I wanted. That's a lot of

extra time for playing soccer, inventing computer games, and making up new math puzzles.

The grid on the back of the transport cubes made it easy for us to navigate our way around the city. Lexie and I have used grids like that in math before, so we already knew how they worked. When our family took a car trip to my grandmother's house last summer, my parents put me in charge of navigation. The map I used had a similar grid, too.

If you haven't used a coordinate grid before, they're simple to use. The horizontal line at the bottom is called the *x*-axis, and the vertical line along the side is called the *y*-axis. Coordinates are the two numbers that help you find a spot on the grid.

Here's an example:

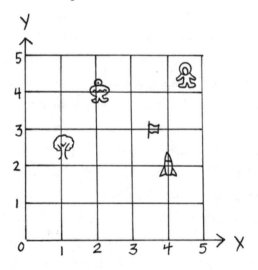

If I wanted to locate the rocket on this grid, I'd start by putting my finger on the 0 (the origin) and slide it horizontally along the *x*-axis till it was directly beneath the

rocket. I'm on the number 4, and that would be my first coordinate. Then I'd slide my finger up till it reached the rocket. It lines up with the 2 on the *y*-axis, and that's my second coordinate. Finally I would write the two numbers in parentheses with a comma between them, like this: (4, 2).

But be careful! Make sure you put the *x*-coordinate first; otherwise you'll get a completely different spot. If I went to the spot (2, 4) instead of (4, 2), I'd end up at the angry alien. Not a good idea, especially since he looks like he's in a bad mood. It's easy to remember which coordinate comes first: *x* always comes before *y* in the alphabet, so the *x*-coordinate always comes before the *y*-coordinate on a grid. Or you can remember that you always move horizontally first, and then vertically, by thinking: you go *into* a house before you climb *up* the stairs.

All of the transport cubes on the map were located exactly at the intersection of two lines. That made it simple to plot their coordinates. But what happens when you want to find a point that *doesn't* land exactly at an intersection, such as the tree on this map? That's simple, too. You just use a decimal, or fraction, to show that it is partway between two numbers. The tree lines up with 1 on the *x*-axis, so its first coordinate is 1. But it's halfway between 2 and 3 on the *y*-axis, so its second coordinate would be 2.5 (or 2½). That means the coordinates for the tree are (1, 2.5).

Can you figure out the coordinates for the flag? And the coordinates for the person? If you said (3.5, 3) and (4.5, 4.5), you're ready to join our math team!

Mystery Picture

I made up a test to challenge your point-plotting skills. It'll test your drawing skills, too.

First, you'll need a piece of lined graph paper, or you can draw a grid like the one below. Label the *x*-axis and *y*-axis, and number the lines on each axis from 0 to 9.

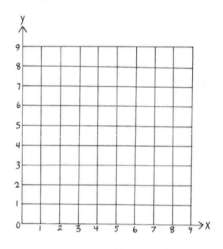

Next, plot the following pairs of coordinates on the grid. As you plot each point, connect it with a line segment to the previous point that you made, like you're making a dot-to-dot picture. Remember, the *x*-coordinate always comes first!

1. (2, 7)	6. (7, 6)	11. (5, 1)	16. (2, 4)
2. (3, 9)	7. (7, 8)	12. (6, 0)	17. (0, 3)
3. (5, 9)	8. (8, 5)	13. (2, 0)	18. (2, 5)
4. (6, 7)	9. (6, 4)	14. (3, 1)	19. (2, 7)
5. (6, 5)	10. (6, 2)	15. (2, 2)	

Now, on the same grid, start over and plot these points, connecting them as you go, to make a brand-new shape. This time you'll have to use some "halfway" coordinates.

1. (3, 2)
2. (3, 3.5)
3. (4, 4.5)
4. (5, 3.5)
5. (5, 2)
6. (4, 1.5)
7. (3, 2)

Start over one more time and make this last shape, once again connecting the dots with line segments:

1. (4, 5)
2. (3.5, 7.5)
3. (4.5, 7.5)
4. (4, 5)

To finish your drawing, plot these final two points, but DON'T connect them this time!

(3, 8)
(5, 8)

You're done! Do you recognize who you just drew? You can compare your drawing to my masterpiece at the end of my notebook.

How to Paint a Satellite

When Lexie and I were looking for the box with the communicators, one of the clues in Zell's note told us to find a building with floor space that was exactly three square units in area.

Area is how much space a flat shape covers. It was easy to figure out the area of most of the buildings on the map. We just counted the number of squares they covered. For example, building SLZ covered twelve squares, so its area was twelve square units.

But we could have also figured out its area by multiplying its length (six squares) by its width (two squares):

6 squares × 2 squares = 12 square units

That's quicker than counting, especially when you've got a really big shape. It's also handy because most shapes aren't divided into squares like they were on the map. For example, last spring our school decided to cover the playing area of the soccer field with new sod. But before they could buy the sod, they needed to

know the area of the field. Can you guess who they asked to find the area? The school's awesome math team!

We didn't have to draw squares on the field to find the area (although that would have looked pretty cool). All we did was measure its length and its width, then multiply:

Area of soccer field:

100 yards × 60 yards = 6,000 square yards

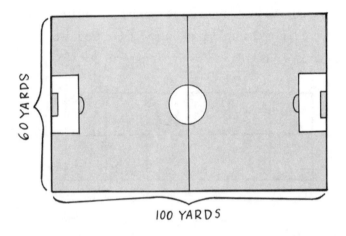

But not every shape is a rectangle like a soccer field. That's when finding the area can get tricky. It's also more challenging, which I like.

Last summer my parents told me I could paint my bedroom wall whatever color I wanted. That was a no-brainer. I chose electric lime green, my all-time favorite color.

Before we went to the paint store, I had to figure out how much paint I needed. To do that, I needed to know the area of the wall. This is what my wall looks like. I only had to paint the wall, not the door:

How did I figure out its area when my wall isn't a perfect rectangle?

Easy.

First I divided the wall into three imaginary rectangles, then I found the area of each of those smaller rectangles. Finally I added the area of the three small rectangles together to get the area of the entire wall.

Rectangle A = 7 feet × 9 feet
= 63 square feet

Rectangle B = 3 feet × 2 feet
= 6 square feet

Rectangle C = 2 feet × 9 feet
= 18 square feet

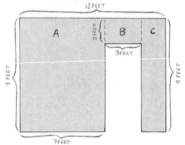

Total area of my bedroom wall: 63 square feet + 6 square feet + 18 square feet = 87 square feet

Did you notice that I didn't have the measurement for the short side of Rectangle C? But I was still able to figure it out anyway. I knew that the entire length of my wall was twelve feet, and that Rectangle A took up seven feet and Rectangle B took up three feet. That left two feet for the side of Rectangle C that I was missing. I love figuring out puzzles like that!

When Lexie heard I was going to paint my bedroom

wall, she asked her father if she could paint her wall, too. Not electric lime green. *Her* favorite color is ocean-morning blue. Her bedroom is the same shape as mine, but she figured out the area of her wall using a completely different way.

First she figured out the area of the entire wall, *including* the door. Then she subtracted the area of the door, because she didn't have to paint that part.

Entire wall: 12 feet × 9 feet = 108 square feet

Door: 3 feet × 7 feet = 21 square feet

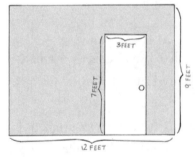

Total area of Lexie's bedroom wall: 108 square feet – 21 square feet = 87 square feet

Pretty clever, huh? One of the things I like about math is that you can get the same answer to a problem using a completely different strategy.

Now it's *your* turn. Imagine that you've been hired by an intergalactic painting company to paint the sides of their new satellites. Here are three shapes they want you to paint:

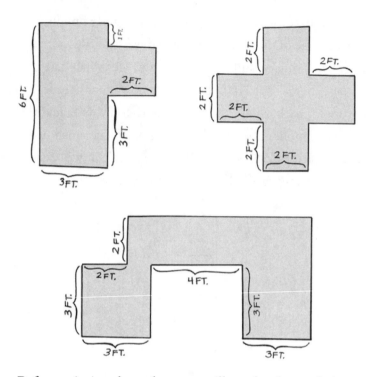

Before painting these shapes, you'll need to know their areas so you can be sure to bring enough paint. You'll have to divide them into smaller rectangles to get your answers, and you've only been given *some* of the measurements for each shape. Can you still figure out the area of each one?

Not all the shapes on the map of Naznar could be divided into rectangles, but we were still able to find their areas anyway. For a shape like building UTZ, we just added the whole squares and half squares together.

½ square + ½ square + 1 square = 2 square units

But for other buildings, like the triangular building ZMC, some of the squares it covered were a little more than half a square, and some were a little less than half a square. It was hard to know exactly how much area it covered. That's when I remembered what my dad taught me about finding the area of a triangle. When I imagined that the shape ZMC was a half of a rectangle, it was easy to see that its area was half its length times its width.

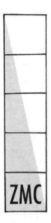

Total area of the rectangle:
1 square × 5 squares = 5 square units

Total area of the shaded triangular building ZMC is half the area of the rectangle: 2½ square units. My dad told me this works for all triangles. Here's the formula he gave me:

Area of a triangle = (base × height) ÷ 2

The *base* is the flat part the triangle sits on, and the *height* is how tall it is from the base to its highest point.

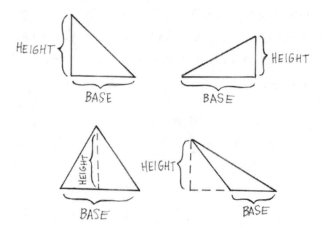

The base of this triangle is four inches and its height is five inches. So that means its area is:

$$(4 \text{ inches} \times 5 \text{ inches}) \div 2$$

or

$$20 \text{ square inches} \div 2$$

or

$$10 \text{ square inches}$$

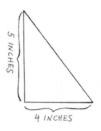

It's your turn again. You did such a good job painting the satellites, you've been promoted. Now the intergalactic painting company is sending you to its new space station to

paint three of its floors. You'll have to divide each shape into rectangles *and* triangles to find their areas. Can you do it? Don't give up . . . or they'll hire an alien from another planet to do the job!

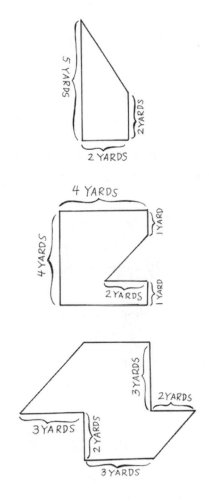

You can check your answers with mine at the end of my notebook.

Count Like a Roman

I'd love to have a pen that writes in glowing ink like the pen Zell used to write the Roman numerals in her note. I like making secret messages . . . and I like Roman numerals, too. They're like mini–math puzzles.

Roman numerals use these seven letters:

$$I = 1$$
$$V = 5$$
$$X = 10$$
$$L = 50$$
$$C = 100$$
$$D = 500$$
$$M = 1,000$$

If you have trouble remembering the order of the letters, here's something that Mrs. Nguyen, the coach of our math team, taught us. Think of the sentence:

I Value Xylophones Like Cows Do Milk.

The first letter in each word gives you the seven Roman numerals in order from the smallest to the largest: I, V, X, L, C, D, M.

To make other numbers besides those seven, you combine the letters together. For example:

$$III = 1 + 1 + 1 = 3$$

$$XV = 10 + 5 = 15$$

$$DCLI = 500 + 100 + 50 + 1 = 651$$

It's pretty easy. But here comes the tricky part. You'd think that you'd write 4 in Roman numerals as IIII (1 + 1 + 1 + 1). But you don't. Instead, there's a shortcut so you don't have to write so many letters.

Instead of using addition and writing all those I's, you use subtraction and write IV, which means 1 less than 5. This shortcut means that you won't have to use the same Roman numeral more than three times in a row.

So, how do you know when to use subtraction and when to use addition when reading Roman numerals? That's the part that's like a mini–math puzzle. If a smaller Roman numeral comes before a larger Roman numeral, that's your clue to subtract the smaller number from the bigger number.

IX means 1 less than 10 = 9

XC means 10 less than 100 = 90

CD means 100 less than 500 = 400

Here's a test: Can you tell which of the numbers below is 49 and which is 51?

IL   LI

IL is 49 because the smaller number I comes before the bigger number L.

IL means 1 less than 50 = 49

LI means 50 + 1 = 51

When Lexie and I went to the city library last week we noticed that the year the library was built was chiseled

in stone at the bottom of the building. (If you start looking at buildings around town, you'll notice that a lot of them have the date they were built chiseled in Roman numerals.) This is what we saw carved in the block of stone by the library's front door:

MCMLXIV

We wanted to know what year that meant, so we began decoding the date letter by letter. We had to watch when a smaller number came before a larger number so that we'd know when we had to use subtraction.

MCMLXIV

M = 1,000

C (100) is less than M (1,000), so CM means 100 less than 1,000 = 900:

L = 50

X = 10

I (1) is less than V (5), so IV means 1 less than 5 = 4:

MCMLXIV = 1,000 + 900 + 50 + 10 + 4 = 1964

I was still thinking about Roman numerals when we got inside the library. I noticed that some of the books on display had numbers in their titles, so I made a list of what their titles would look like using Roman numerals instead. Then I showed the list to Lexie. She was able to decode them all. How about you?

Snow White and the VII Dwarfs
The D Hats of Bartholomew Cubbins
The CI Dalmatians
Around the World in LXXX Days
MI Arabian Nights
The Watsons Go to Birmingham, MCMLXIII
The XIVth Goldfish
Ramona Quimby, Age VIII

I saw another book with the title *20,000 Leagues Under the Sea*. But the largest Roman numeral is M. M stands for 1,000. Did that mean for 20,000, I'd have to write: MMMMMMMMMMMMMMMMMMMM? That seemed crazy.

At school the next day I asked Mrs. Nguyen. She told me that if you write a bar over the top of a Roman numeral, it means multiply that number by 1,000. So . . .

$$\overline{V} \text{ means } 5 \times 1,000 = 5,000$$

$$\overline{X} \text{ means } 10 \times 1,000 = 10,000$$

$$\overline{L} \text{ means } 50 \times 1,000 = 50,000$$

If I wanted to write 20,000, I could write it as $\overline{XX}$. That's a lot easier than writing twenty M's!

And for really, *really* big numbers, Mrs. Nguyen said you draw an open box around the number, which means multiply that number by 100,000:

$$\overline{|V|} \text{ means } 5 \times 100,000 = 500,000$$

$\boxed{\text{X}}$ means 10 × 100,000 = 1,000,000

$\boxed{\text{L}}$ means 50 × 100,000 = 5,000,000

That afternoon I hunted around our neighborhood and apartment for things that had Roman numerals on them. I looked for XXIV minutes and found VI different things. Can you read all the numbers I found?

I could *not*, however, find a super-big Roman numeral that had a bar on top of it or box around it. Maybe someday there will be a Super Bowl $\boxed{\text{X}}$, but until then, if you find a Roman numeral for a gigantic number, let me know!

It's About Time

The Chronok that the penguins gave us was a pretty strange way to measure time. Then again, penguins measuring time at all seems pretty weird.

People on Earth have used unusual clocks, too. In 1791, my favorite mathematician, Benjamin Banneker, made a mechanical clock entirely out of wood using only his pocketknife. It kept accurate time for over *forty* years! You can read how he built his clock in a book called *Ticktock Banneker's Clock* by Shana Keller, illustrated by David Gardner.

I started looking on the Internet for other unusual clocks. These are some of the ones I found.

Sundials are a type of clock that people have been using for a long, long time. They measure time based on where the sun's shadow lands throughout the day. You can still sometimes find sundials in parks and gardens. (Our city park has a huge metal sundial in the middle of the rose garden.) One good thing about sundials is that they don't need electricity or batteries; on the other hand, they're pretty useless on a cloudy day . . . or at night.

Candle clocks measure time according to how fast a candle melts. The stem of the candle is marked in segments that keep track of how much time passes. There have even been candle alarm clocks! A nail is stuck into

the side of the candle at a specific point, and when the wax melts to that point, the nail falls out and—*bang!*—hits a metal plate below. If my older brother used a candle alarm clock, he would need a *gigantic* nail to wake him up. Candle clocks were useful because they worked at night and on cloudy days . . . but *not* if the wind blew out the flame.

Water clocks measure time according to how long it takes water to drain through a hole from one container to another. Some of these water clocks were big. And I mean BIG. Almost a thousand years ago, a man named Su Sung in China designed an elaborate water clock with moving mannequins that was over thirty feet tall! You couldn't keep a watch like that in your pocket!

Hourglasses and sand timers measure time according to how long it takes sand to empty from one glass bulb (on top) to another (on the bottom). They've been handy because you can use them at night and on cloudy days, and they are small enough to carry from one room to another. My dad still uses a three-minute sand timer when he makes a soft-boiled egg. I asked him once why he didn't use the stopwatch app on his phone instead. He told me, "This timer belonged to my grandfather. It's one of the ways that I honor his memory." Then he winked and added, "Besides, sometimes it's fun to do things the old-fashioned way."

The most accurate clocks now are atomic clocks. They're powered by the vibrations of atoms. They are so accurate that they won't gain or lose a second in *billions* of years! That's a lot more accurate than a candle clock or sand timer.

I don't know how to make an atomic clock, at least not yet, but I *was* able to make my own sand timer. You can, too.

These are the things you will need:

- Two identical empty plastic bottles (I used empty water bottles. Make sure they are *completely* dry inside, or the sand or sugar will clump together.)
- One or two cups of sugar (I wanted to use real sand, but the sand at the local playground was full of stones and twigs. Unless you live near a beach with fine, clean sand, or unless you buy some sand at a craft store, you'll have better luck if you use sugar. But ask your parents first. You don't want them getting mad when they discover there's no sugar left for their coffee!)
- Tape (Clear packaging tape works best, but duct tape works well, too.)

Start by having an adult help you make a hole in the cap of one of the plastic bottles. This is the hardest part of the whole project, and you don't want to accidentally get hurt. My mom and I used a ¾-inch drill to make the hole. The hole was *about* this big:

●

If you make the hole too small, the sugar won't flow through it; if you make the hole too big, the sugar will flow too fast.

Fill one of the empty bottles about half full with sugar (or sand). It's easier if you use a funnel. I used about one cup of sugar.

Screw the cap with the hole onto the bottle with the sugar. You won't need to use the other cap.

Place the empty bottle (without a cap) on top of the first, with the two tops facing each other, as shown at the right.

Tape them together securely (you don't want sugar leaking out all over the place).

Flip the bottles over and watch the sugar pour from one bottle to the next. Use a watch to time exactly how long it takes for the top bottle to empty into the bottom one. You can adjust the length of time by changing the amount of sugar.

Did you know that there is a sand timer in Japan that is seventeen feet tall and uses a *ton* of sand? It takes exactly one *year* for the top bulb to empty.

My timer takes only about two minutes to empty. Lexie and I use it for a game we invented called Frantic Five! Here's how it works:

One player flips the timer over.

The other player rolls five dice and then adds the amounts shown on the faces together as quickly as possible. She announces the total, and rolls again.

Score one point for every time the player can roll and add the dice before the timer runs out. Then switch places so that the other person gets a chance to be the player rolling and adding the dice.

So far, Lexie holds the record with twenty-five rolls before running out of time, but she'd better watch out. I've been practicing and I plan to smash her record the next time we play.

Try playing Frantic Five! with the timer that you made . . . or try inventing your own game.

Models Make It Easier

Sometimes it's easier and faster to solve a math problem by working it out in your head. But other times it's not.

Both Lexie and I are smart, but it would have been tough to figure out the way to measure one Veng of Smoo just by *thinking* about it. It was easier when we could experiment by pouring the Smoo back and forth between the different containers and seeing the results. We didn't get the right answer on our first try, but that was okay. Mrs. Nguyen always tells us that it doesn't mean we've failed if we have to start over again. It just means we've eliminated one wrong answer and we're that much closer to finding the solution.

After a lot of trial and error, Lexie and I *did* find the solution to measuring one Veng of Smoo . . . and we saved Fooz from remaining a statue forever.

Here's a math problem that Mrs. Nguyen gave us at one of our practice meets:

You have a piece of cloth that is nine feet long by seven feet wide. You want to cut it into flags that are 2 feet × 3 feet in size. Without sewing scraps together, what is the most number of flags you can make?

It doesn't sound at all like the problem of measuring Smoo, but our math team solved it the same way. We used a model to experiment with different solutions. No, we didn't get a gigantic piece of cloth and start cutting it up into flags. Instead, we drew a piece of cloth on paper and divided it into a 9 × 7 grid.

Next, we cut little pieces of paper that each covered 2 × 3 squares to represent the flags.

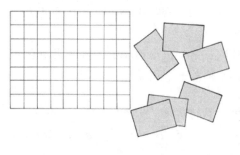

Then we tried arranging the flags in different ways to see how many we could fit onto the grid.

Here's our first try. We were only able to fit eight flags onto the grid. We all knew we could do better than that.

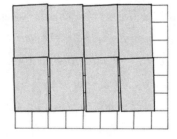

On our second try, we were able to fit nine flags on the grid, but there was still a lot of unused space. We still thought we could do better, so we kept trying.

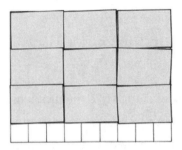

After more trial and error, we finally found a way to fit ten flags on the grid. Can you figure out how we did it? And can you tell how we were certain that this was the most flags possible?

Everyone on our team agreed that it was easier to use a model to solve the problem than if we just had tried to picture the problem in our heads.

After Lexie and I got home from our trip to Zan (and after we ate brownies), I made up a math problem:

Four penguins from the planet Pengolia were exploring a dark cave. They came to an old rickety bridge that could hold only 100 pounds at a time. One of the penguins weighed 99 pounds, two of the penguins weighed 50 pounds each, and the last penguin weighed 49 pounds. Because it was so dark, they needed to carry a flashlight with them every time they crossed the bridge. The flashlight weighed 1 pound.

How can all the penguins cross the bridge without it collapsing?

If the problem seems tough, try doing what Lexie did. She made a model to help her solve it.

Draw four penguins on scraps of paper, and label each one with how much it weighs.

Draw a flashlight on another scrap of paper, and label how much it weighs.

Now draw a long bridge.

Place all the penguins and the flashlight on one side of the bridge. Start moving them across the bridge. Remember, the bridge can never hold more than 100 pounds at a time and the penguins always have to carry the flashlight, which weighs one pound (and no, they can't throw the flashlight across the bridge, or it will break).

Don't worry: if you get stuck, just start over again.

Once you've solved that problem, here's a trickier one:

Those same four penguins finished exploring and were ready to leave the cave. They came back to that same bridge, but one of the fifty-pound penguins had been eating fish from an underground pool and now weighed fifty-one pounds.

Can you still get all four penguins across?

Use a model to help you, and don't give up! The penguins of Pengolia are counting on you!

LAMAR'S NOTEBOOK
Answers to Lamar's Puzzles

TOP SECRET!

Don't peek without trying my puzzles first!

On the Grid:

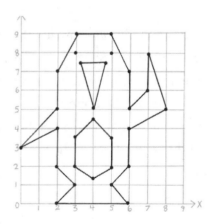

It's King Pong!

How to Paint a Satellite

This is how I divided these shapes to calculate their areas. Maybe you divided them a different way to get the same answers. I've also included the missing dimensions. How many of the areas were you able to figure out?

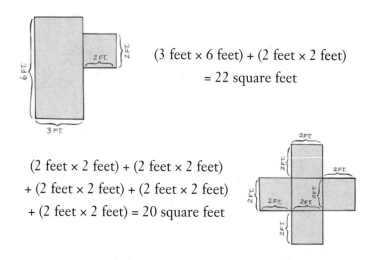

(3 feet × 6 feet) + (2 feet × 2 feet)
= 22 square feet

(2 feet × 2 feet) + (2 feet × 2 feet)
+ (2 feet × 2 feet) + (2 feet × 2 feet)
+ (2 feet × 2 feet) = 20 square feet

First I figured out the area of the giant rectangle. Then I subtracted the areas of the smaller rectangles:

(10 feet × 5 feet) – (2 feet × 2 feet) – (4 feet × 3 feet) =
34 square feet

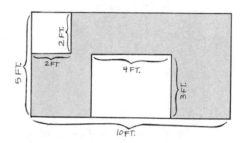

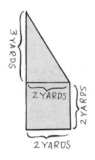

[(2 yards × 3 yards) ÷ 2] + (2 yards × 2 yards)
= 7 square yards

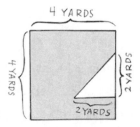

First I figured out the area of the square. Then I subtracted the area of the triangle:

(4 yards × 4 yards) − [(2 yards × 2 yards) ÷ 2]
= 14 square yards

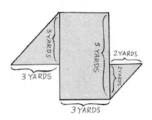

[(3 yards × 3 yards) ÷ 2] + (3 yards × 5 yards) +
[(2 yards × 2 yards) ÷ 2] = 21½ square yards

Count Like a Roman

These are the titles of the books I saw at the library:

Snow White and the Seven Dwarfs
The 500 Hats of Bartholomew Cubbins
The Hundred and One Dalmatians
Around the World in Eighty Days
One Thousand and One Arabian Nights
The Watsons Go to Birmingham, 1963
The Fourteenth Goldfish
Ramona Quimby, Age 8

The books looked so good, Lexie and I have been checking them out and reading them. Between the II of us, we've already read VI of the books, and we've liked C percent of them!

Here are the decoded Roman numerals I found around my neighborhood and apartment:

Chapter 29 in a book

A pennant for Mega Bowl 54

The movie *Attack of the Worms 8* (Don't watch it if you're having spaghetti for dinner!)

Don's Donuts established in 1990 (Yum! Their blueberry-glazed donuts are the best!)

This statue to the city's first librarian was dedicated in 1866.

My dad's 15th volume of *Famous Mathematicians* (look for my name and Lexie's name in a future volume)

Models Make It Easier

This is the solution our math team came up with for Mrs. Nguyen's flag puzzle. (Your solution might look different than ours.)

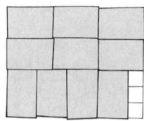

We knew we couldn't fit more than ten flags on the grid because there isn't enough cloth left over to make an eleventh flag.

Someone on our math team suggested that instead of making a model, we could have solved this problem by just finding the area of the big piece of cloth and dividing it by the area of one of the flags:

Area of the big piece of cloth = 63 square feet

Area of one of the flags = 6 square feet

63 ÷ 6 = 10 flags with a remainder of 3 square feet of cloth

That *looked* like a good strategy until Mrs. Nguyen gave us this new problem:

You have a piece of cloth that is five feet long by five feet wide. You want to cut it into flags that are three feet by three feet in size. Without sewing scraps together, what is the most number of flags you can make?

When we tried the dividing strategy, we got:

Area of the big piece of cloth = 25 square feet

Area of one of the flags = 9 square feet

25 ÷ 9 = 2 flags, with a remainder of 7 square feet of cloth

But when we made a model, we saw immediately it was impossible to cut two 3 foot × 3 foot flags from a piece of cloth that was 5 feet × 5 feet.

Make a model yourself, and you'll see why!

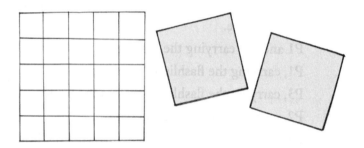

And here are the solutions for my Penguins on the Bridge puzzle. I numbered the penguins like this to make it easier for me to write my solution:

P1 = 49-pound penguin

P2 = 50-pound penguin

P3 = 50-pound penguin

P4 = 99-pound penguin

P1, P2, P3, P4, and the flashlight start at one end of the bridge.

P1 and P2, carrying the flashlight, cross the bridge.

P1, carrying the flashlight, goes back.

P1 and P3, carrying the flashlight, cross the bridge.

P1, carrying the flashlight, goes back.

$6.95 U.S.
$9.50 CAN.

Best friends Lexie and Lamar love math—

and in this second book in the Alien Math series, their skills come in handy when they head off on another journey to help their space alien friend, Fooz. It seems the extraterrestrial's planet has been overrun with penguins. These invading creatures may look adorable, but they terrify inhabitants who turn to stone whenever they see even the tiniest baby penguin. To help their friend and save the aliens, Lamar and Lexie must solve a series of puzzles that require reading map coordinates, interpreting Roman numerals, and measuring time. Test *your* wits as you try to solve the same type of puzzles the two friends tackle as they face the mighty wrath of King Pong and his penguins in this math-filled outer-space adventure!

ALSO AVAILABLE:

STERLING CHILDREN'S BOOKS
New York

ISBN 978-1-4549-2922-2

9 781454 929222

5 0 6 9 5 >

Manufactured in Canada